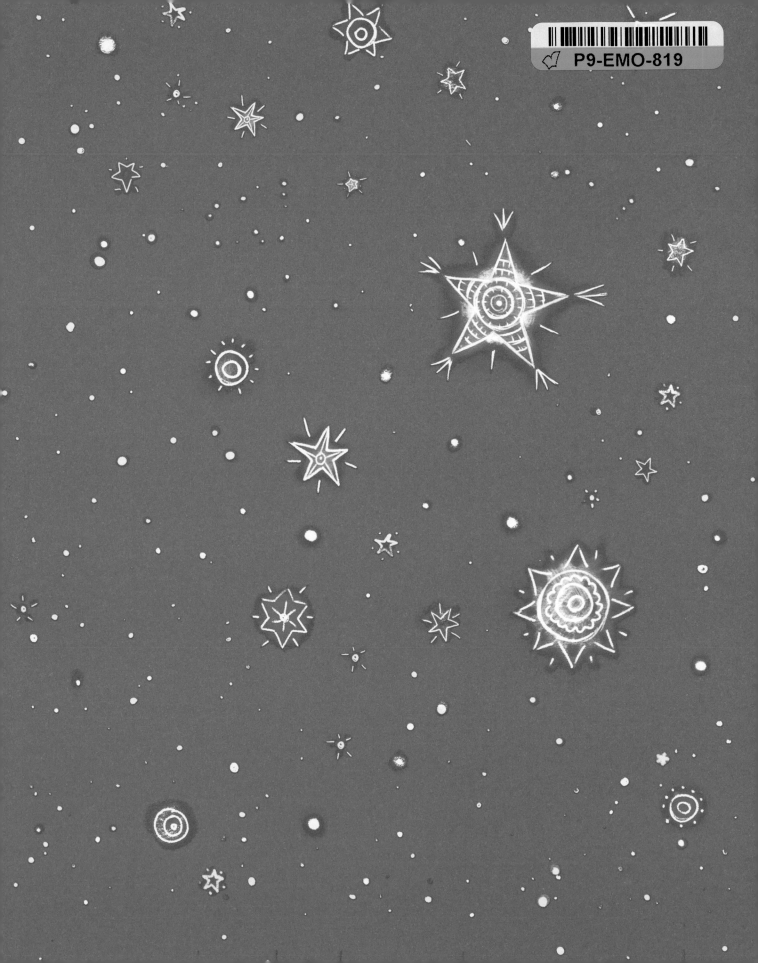

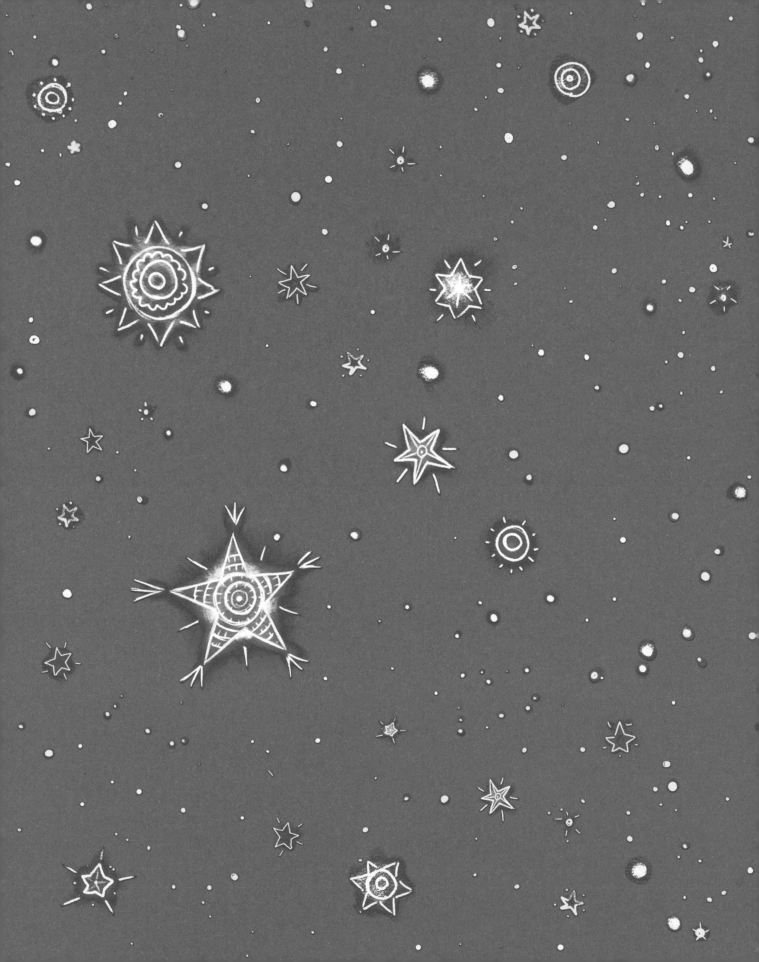

WITH LOTS OF LOVE

Written by JENNY TORRES SANCHEZ

Illustrated by ANDRÉ CEOLIN

VIKING

VIKING

An imprint of Penguin Random House LLC, New York

First published in the United States of America by Viking, an imprint of Penguin Random House LLC, 2022

Text copyright © 2022 by Jenny Torres Sanchez
Illustrations copyright © 2022 by André Ceolin

Viking & colophon are registered trademarks of Penguin Random House LLC.

Visit us online at penguinrandomhouse.com.

Library of Congress Cataloging-in-Publication Data is available.

Manufactured in Spain

ISBN 9780593205006

10 9 8 7 6 5 4 3 2 1

EST

Edited by Liza Kaplan
Design by Ellice M. Lee
Text set in P22 Mayflower

Art done in Krita and Adobe Photoshop.

For Francesca, mi estrellita.
And for anyone who has ever missed someone.
—J. T. S.

For my family and for those who feel at
home while watching the stars.
—A. C.

Rocio had a new home.

But she really missed her other home.
The little house where she used to live
with Abuela, Tía Rosa, and her cousins.

She missed Abuela's small grocery store, where her grandmother sold fresh fruits and vegetables, pan dulce, and ice pops made of watermelon, mango, and coconut cream.

Rocio used to visit Abuela's store every day.
Abuela always called out, "Hola, mi amor!"
Her voice sounded like a faraway flute.

Sometimes Rocio closed her eyes and pretended she was back at Abuela's store. The smell of spicy peppers and burnt sugar danced in her nose. And Abuela's gentle voice played in her ears.

She could hear, too, the soft rustling of piñatas that hung from the ceiling.

Rocio missed those piñatas that Abuela made herself. How they swayed and whispered every time she walked into the store. And she missed the sweet treats made from marmalade, sweet milk, and fruit that spilled from them at celebrations.

If only she had asked Abuela to make her a piñata to decorate her new room in the United States.

Rocio missed many other things, too . . .

The buñuelos drizzled with honey that Abuela made for everyone. And the extra-sweet coffee that Abuela made just for her.

She missed Abuela's warm tortillas and the way they smelled sweet and fresh, like the damp earth after a soft rain.

She missed the pretty song of her language.

She missed gazing at the blue-black night,

sprinkled with stars, with Abuela at bedtime.

Most of all, she missed Abuela.

Rocio looked up at the nighttime sky from the
window of her new house. It was full of stars, too.

Rocio searched for the brightest
star and made a wish.

In the morning Rocio woke to
Mamá, Papá, her brother, and her
sister singing "Las Mañanitas."

Rocio smiled as they sang about the beauty of the morning she was born. Then Mamá pointed to a box and said, "You got a package in the mail this morning."

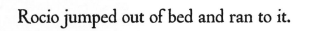
Rocio jumped out of bed and ran to it.

She recognized Abuela's crooked handwriting right away.

Con mucho amor.
"With lots of love."

Inside was a dazzling star made of bright ruffled paper. Shiny streamers hung from its pointed tips. Rocio took it out and her eyes filled with tears.

Con mucho amor

Beneath it she noticed a smaller package.

A cloth towel stitched with Rocio's name. Rocio closed her eyes and held it to her cheek. She smelled a sweet, earthy smell. Inside were tortillas perfectly shaped by Abuela's gentle hands.

Then she noticed
one last gift.

A picture of Abuela, Tía, and her cousins holding a banner
in front of Abuela's grocery store.

¡Feliz Cumpleaños, Rocio!

Rocio kissed the picture
and thought of the star
she had wished on last
night. Abuela had plucked it
from the sky and sent it to her.

That night, the piñata hung above Rocio's bed.
The picture sat on Rocio's nightstand. And
Rocio blew Abuela a good-night kiss.

She watched as it traveled out her window,

through the night sky, past so many stars,

to where it landed, back home,
on Abuela's cheek.

With lots of love.